Violets and Vengeance

A Treehouse Hotel Cozy Mystery (Book 2)

Sue Hollowell

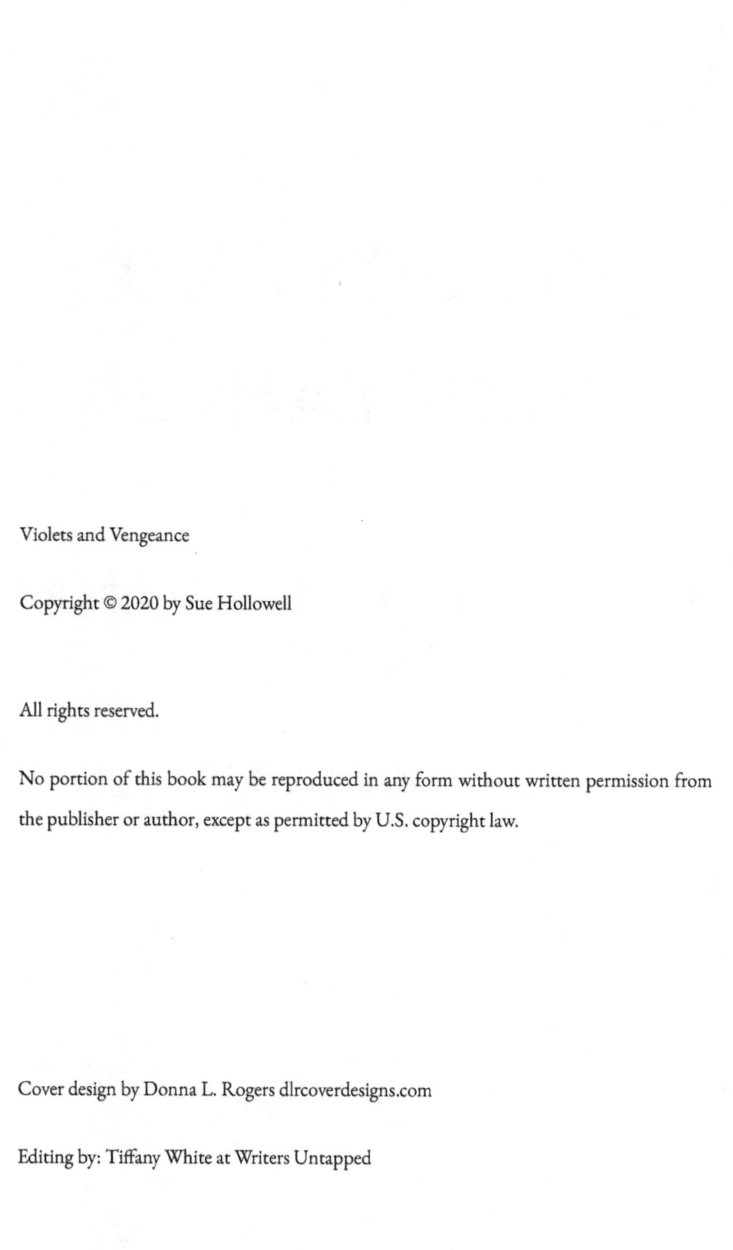

Violets and Vengeance

Cover design by Donna L. Rogers dlrcoverdesigns.com

Editing by: Tiffany White at Writers Untapped

CONTENTS

CHAPTER ONE

Buttercup Bungalow began to look like my vision of what the Cedarbrook Treehouse Hotel could be. Guests should expect staying in a treehouse would be an adventure with fun and whimsy sprinkled in. When I arrived to help Mom untangle the books so we could list the hotel for sale, I never expected to stay this long. My dutiful companion Max and I originally stayed at Mom's when I returned to town. But I needed my space. And staying in a room at the hotel would give me a better chance to renovate it the way it deserved.

The hotel in its prime was a destination for many. Rooms were booked a year in advance. The place was a hub for many functions in this small town. If only I could get it even partially returned to that glory, I'd consider myself successful. I was handy with a toolbelt and not afraid to get my hands dirty. Plus, fixing up the rooms was kind of like solving a puzzle—replacing what's missing, fixing problems—and I'd always been good at puzzles.

Today, I was decorating the interior of this place. I'd gone to the stores in Emerald Hills to find yellow-themed items to go along with buttercups. I purchased material with yellow flowers to hang up as curtains and some paint to cover the nightstand in a matching golden hue. The place had already brightened with those two changes. The wooden walls of the treehouses darkened the interior and required creativity to style and lighten it up. I wanted the feel of happiness, joy, and relaxation for all of the units. Spending time with Mom while fixing the place up had become enjoyable. The times we worked together, I appreciated her sense of whimsy. Although she insisted we display some of those garden gnomes she collected. I just couldn't go there.

My phone chimed and I saw Pearl's Pooch Pampering on the caller ID. I'd taken Max and Trixie to get groomed earlier this morning, and it looked like they were calling to let me know they were ready to be picked up. My sister, Joey, one of us triplets, was a part-time cashier there when she wasn't waitressing at Smokehouse Restaurant. She had several family members living with her, so she held down multiple jobs to try and make ends meet.

"Hi, Joey. Are the pooches ready to be picked up?"

Silence on the other end. I thought maybe the connection was bad. Out here at the hotel, sometimes reception was spotty, at best.

"Joey? Can you hear me?" I heard sniffles. "Joey, is that you?"

"Chloe, you won't believe it," she said and sniffled.

At least we had a connection now. And yes, I probably would believe it. My time in Cedarbrook had been more than eventful. Edna's murder had thrown this place into a tizzy. And with that resolved, the excitement began to disappear. Plus, out of all my siblings, Joey had the most drama. She had quite a few kids and grandkids, and someone or another was always in trouble. Bless her heart, though, she always retained a positive outlook, no matter how many times she had to bail someone out of jail.

"What's going on? Are the pups ready to be picked up?" My faithful companion, Max, had fur that went on for days. His buff-colored cocker spaniel coat needed constant care or we'd be in for a rat's nest like no other. Sticks and leaves adhered to him like Velcro. Sometimes when I peeled them off I had a pile of debris the size of a small shrub. Trixie was new to our family. When Mom's friend Edna died, her boyfriend didn't want to keep the little dog. She was a bit of a handful, but her companionship was unparalleled. I'd taken her for a bit while we sorted things out with Edna, and by the end of that time, Trixie and Mom had become fast friends. To say I was shocked was an understatement. That Trixie could soften Mom's demeanor was truly amazing. Now Mom rarely went anywhere without her.

"No," Joey said. This was like pulling teeth.

"Is it Mom?" I asked. Mom was in her eighties. She retained great health for that age, just had the usual aches and pains of an older body.

"No. It's Violet," she said. Violet and Joey had no love lost between them. But really, anyone in town could say that about themselves and Violet.

"Did you guys get into it again?" I asked. Silence. I was sure I'd lost the connection now. I looked at my phone and saw surprisingly we were still getting a pretty strong signal. It was about time to head to Pearl's anyway to get the dogs. It was a good time for a break from all of the buttercup yellow, as cheery as that was. "Joey, I'll be there soon." I listened for a few seconds and didn't hear a disconnect.

"Chloe." Joey started crying even more. "I don't know what happened."

I beelined out the door to my car. Pearl was owner of the dog spa and had a pretty level head. "Is Pearl there?"

"I don't know where she is. She went on an errand but wouldn't say what it was."

Clearly I wasn't going to get any more information from Joey on the call. I threw my purse onto the passenger seat and started the car. "I'm on my way."

Pearl's Pooch Pampering was located on the main street of this small town. Rows of quaint little shops lined both sides of the road. Pearl's was pretty much smack dab in the center. Most stores didn't have lots of parking, but you didn't need much in a town with a population of two thousand. Pearl's was no exception. With the amount of business she did, she had tried to expand, but it infringed on the neighboring businesses and was a no-go. Her shop was packed every day. Pet pampering must be a billion-dollar industry, based on how well Pearl did. I found a spot a few blocks away and speed-walked to Pearl's, preparing myself for the unexpected. I heard raised voices before I even got to the front door. The scene through the glass door did not look right. I slowly opened the door. Joey sat in a chair along the wall in the waiting room, her head down, sobbing into a handful of tissues. On the opposite side of the room, Judy, Violet's sister-in-law, was on the phone. She posed business-like in her standard matching pantsuit. We made eye contact and she told the person on the other end of the line she had to go. I wondered what business Judy had here. She was proudly a cat person and let everyone know it. Mom had said the last time her friend Caroline was at Judy's for dinner, her felines even sat at the table and ate off of plates.

"Chloe, Violet's dead," Judy proclaimed. She gestured to the other side of the large display of pet supplies.

My hand flew to my mouth. "Oh my God! What happened?" I asked the room. I'd take an explanation from anyone right now. Violet's body was situated on her left side, facing the wall, her head covered by stuffed plushy dog toys.

"Were you calling an ambulance?" I asked Judy, and navigated to the chair next to Joey.

"What good would that do?" Judy replied as she paced. Judy glanced at Joey, paused, then said, "I found her like that when I came in."

Joey looked up, obviously distraught. "I heard the bell ring and thought it was Violet coming to get Sasha. You know she griped every time about how we trimmed her poodle. And she thought the prices were outrageous for what she was getting. I just couldn't take it anymore." Joey dipped her head again. She extended her left arm toward Violet. "I came into the room and found Judy standing over Violet."

My heart sank. I'd never known Joey to be violent. But I guess we never truly knew what people could do under pressure.

I sat next to Joey and grabbed her hand. "Joey," I said, locking into her gaze. My shoulders slumped.

She shook her head no. I would have to take her word for it until I knew the truth. "Where's Sasha now?"

She pointed to the back through a swinging door.

"Judy, would you call Buzz and let him know what happened? He'll want to know someone died in his wife's place of business," I said, taking charge of the mayhem. Buzz was our retired town cop. He would get the investigative ball rolling.

Without a word, she pulled her phone out and dialed.

I headed to the back room to locate Sasha, Trixie, and Max, and make sure the place was still standing. They were all chillin' post-grooming from a day at the spa. Max and Trixie sprinted toward me and Sasha continued to lounge. That was good. We'd have to figure out a home for her now. I grabbed the leashes and led my two dogs back to the lobby, skirting the crime scene.

Judy remained on the phone, but it didn't sound like a call to Buzz. She was a busy person, given her position on the town council.

Max sat and refused to budge. "Max, let's go." His soulful brown eyes looked at me with empathy. "I know, boy. We have quite the puzzle on our hands again." Following Max's lead, Trixie lined up right next to him and plopped down.

CHAPTER TWO

The bell on the front door jingled, startling all of us out of our skin. I turned my attention away from Violet to see who joined the fray.

"What's going on?" Pearl had returned from her errand to find the lobby of the dog spa in disarray and a dead body front and center. She stopped just inside the door, looked at me, then looked down at Violet. Her puppy paw earrings swung from side to side.

I tightened my rein on Max's and Trixie's leashes. "I don't exactly know. Judy called Buzz so he can let the police know she arrived in the lobby and found Violet like she is now." It looked like she took a nosedive into the display of dog toys.

Pearl crossed over to Violet and bent down to get a better view. She looked at me again, as if I magically had the answers to the obvious questions. "Where's Sasha?" she said, looking around.

"She's in the back," I said. "I'll wait here until Buzz arrives."

"Whew." Pearl swiped her forehead. "I'm glad she's OK. From day one when Violet bought that poodle, I've been concerned about her welfare. I'd never forgive myself if something happened to that dog on Violet's watch," Pearl said. "She never treated her like the royal pedigree she is."

Judy crossed the room and stood over Violet. "Pearl, we need to talk about the pet parade. Now that I see Violet's out of the way, I think you should take over as the organizer."

Pearl took a seat next to Joey and grabbed her hand. She looked up and frowned. Not a word. The nerve of Judy to carry on in the midst of this tragedy.

"Judy, seriously," I said. "There's just been a death in Pearl's place of business. Can't we postpone this until another time? Obviously, we have more pressing issues to take care of."

Judy moved to the lobby seats. "No, it can't wait," she snapped. "It's one of the biggest events in this town. And we can't postpone talking about it."

Max sidled up to me and sat on my foot. He began furiously scratching his left side. I reached down and placed my hand on him to stop. His heart raced at the same speed as mine. Trixie nonchalantly selected dog toys that surrounded the body one by one and placed them in a pile by the door. That little girl behaved as if she was entitled to everything.

Pearl stood. "I agree with Chloe. I can't think of anything else right now." She groaned and lifted both hands to cover her face. "Having a dead body in my lobby is going to be horrible for business. I never liked Violet, but I wouldn't wish her dead."

Judy looked at her watch and tapped it. "I have to go. Council business calls. I agree that it's horrible that Violet's dead. But the timing couldn't be better." She sighed, like she was ready to be done with the whole thing. "I mean with you in charge, it will bring so much more dignity to our annual pet parade. Violet always had those hairbrained ideas that made Cedarbrook a laughingstock of the county. People would come to the parade just to see how outrageous it became each year. Kids and their animals dressed up each year and wound their way through town. How dignified could it get?"

Joey stood, having gained some composure, and re-entered the conversation. "Where were you when I needed you? You know that every time Violet comes in she wants to argue with me. When you're here, at least you can handle it. I don't get paid enough to take her crap."

Pearl took three steps back, her hands raised in defense. "I had an important errand to run. And it's none of your business. I pay you plenty to be the cashier. I'd think you would be grateful for the job, with your family and all."

Wow, Pearl took direct aim. Joey's chin trembled, and her head bowed. The tension escalated. Now, they both started crying. Pearl went to Joey and enveloped her in a hug. "I'm sorry. I'm just so stressed over this. It might be the end of my business, just like Violet wanted."

Judy was in her own world. "And for some odd reason, Violet would never allow cats in the parade, only those rambunctious dogs. Cats are so much better behaved. Now I'll be able to show off my Fifi and the others for all the world to see." Judy strutted around the lobby, full of herself now that things were finally going her way.

The bell jingled again, launching us all into the atmosphere. Trixie continued piling up her treasures and had bumped into the door. Oblivious to anything other than her mission, she gripped a little kangaroo in her mouth.

"I should probably get these two out of here," I said. I grabbed their leashes and headed for the exit. "Buzz should be here soon." Trixie refused to leave her pile of treasures. I gave another tug to encourage her departure.

"Chloe, wait." Pearl stretched her arms out to plead for my assistance. "You can't leave me here. You have to help figure out who did this or I'll be ruined. Even dead, Violet's going to take me down."

I didn't have time to help Pearl. Taking care of renovating the treehouses with Mom had become my full-time job.

"Please, Chloe, I'm begging you." Pearl literally clasped her hands in prayer and shook them at me. "You know how hard I've worked to build this business."

Max stood, turned, and looked at me. My little buddy aligned with Pearl in her plea. He smiled that wide grin, confirming we were on the case together. Max looked out for his newfound canine pal Sasha, wanting to help find her mom's killer.

"All right, then," Judy practically yelled. She tucked her phone in her purse and tiptoed passed Trixie to avoid any touching of a dog. "We're all set. Pearl takes over the pet parade. I better go let Otis know what's happened. Even though Violet was his sister, that husband of mine couldn't stand the way she drove that pet parade downhill. Now in his position as grand marshal, he can sit tall and proud, knowing we're representing the county well. Ta, ta, all." Judy skirted out the door and left us all stunned. Judy and Otis were nothing alike. I was surprised they were still together. Otis, our town veterinarian, was a mild-mannered, caring individual with no more aspirations than to care for animals.

"Pearl, I'll wait until Buzz gets here to take over." I looked her in the eye. "Don't worry. We'll get to the bottom of this mystery. It'll be OK," I said with much more conviction than I felt. *Max, we've got to launch our puzzle-solving selves into high gear.*

CHAPTER THREE

I was grateful for the distraction of the morning with some new projects around the hotel. Mom and I were working on renovating Cherry Cottage. This particular unit was a two-story with a loft for additional sleeping, and an expansive wrap-around deck on the main level. I found myself enjoying this time with my mom. We were finding new paths in our relationship, developing a real partnership in running the hotel. After the events of the morning at Pearl's, the pups and I picked Mom up at her house and headed to the treehouses. Since I'd moved from Mom's to the Buttercup Bungalow, my attitude about being in Cedarbrook had significantly improved. It didn't hurt that I was secluded in nature and enjoying puzzle time alone with Max, enjoying my classic huckleberry vodka cocktail and a gorgeous sunset. We screamed through those sudoku challenges like they were nothing.

"Mom, let's work on the outside today. I bought some things at the garden store to get us started." We sat in the two Adirondack chairs in front of the treehouse, finishing lunch I'd picked up at Caroline's.

"Great. I have so many ideas for this one." Max rose from his slumber, stood, and stared at me without blinking. His stubby tail didn't move an inch. *I know, boy. I'm not sure what to expect either.* Mom was a member of the garden club. Her yard was presentable and, dare I say, eclectic. She insisted on collecting garden gnomes galore, and they inhabited most every inch of that space. I hoped one day they'd grow on me, but so far no such luck.

We finished our meals, and I headed to the car to retrieve our supplies. "Why don't we start by potting these flowers and placing them next to the base of the tree?" I lugged flower seedlings, potting soil, and pots to our work area next to the chairs.

Mom returned to my car and rummaged around in the supplies. "What else do you have here?" She took out three garden stakes and held them up and examined them. They were each a little old lady bending over and all you could see were her bloomers showing a pattern of cherries. "I'm not seeing anything interesting. You need to be more creative with the designs if we want people to like them." She reached into the middle row of seats, retrieved a large bag, and returned to our work area.

I started by gloving up and locating the three planters equally spaced on the side of the steps that faced the treehouse. I'd have to get some pictures of the finished project and put them on the website to upgrade the looks of the hotel. We were slowly gaining a few more guests at a time, in no small part due to the upgrades we made.

"Mom, if you want, you can place those garden stakes on the other side of the steps. I think there's three or four of them." Max sauntered over to sniff my work. He looked at Mom, tilted his head to the side where his long ears swung, and straightened his tail. I looked around at Mom as she carried the stakes to their new home. "It's OK, boy. You've had an exciting morning. You deserve some relaxation."

"So tell me again what happened at Pearl's?" Mom was an expert at gossip. When it came time for the garden club meeting, she didn't want to miss a detail in regaling her friends.

I poured soil into the second pot. "All that I know right now is that Violet's dead. Judy said she found her that way. Joey said she found Judy over the body. Pearl wasn't there. Frankly, I don't know what to think at this point."

Mom placed one of the garden stakes and started pounding it with a trowel. Max jolted with the noise and barked. *We're all a bit on edge, boy. It's OK.* I stopped what I was doing and crouched next to him. I grabbed an ear in each hand and gave a massaging knead. He relaxed and sat. Mom continued pounding until the stake was firmly in the ground. I rounded the steps to get a better look.

"That looks great. This is going to really look nice, even with just a few touches here."

Mom stood back to admire her handiwork. "It does look good."

Max approached the stake and gave the old lady's bottom an approving sniff.

"I wish Joey didn't have to work so many jobs. She told me about this guy, Wyatt, who does those housing developments. She said he comes into the restaurant a lot and he's really nice." Mom took a seat in one of the chairs.

I kept filling pots with the soil. "Really? That's nice."

"It would be so great if she married him. He could be the one for her. Of course, this thing with Violet won't help her dating prospects at all." Joey had a few "this is the one" moments already in her life. A bit like Mom. I didn't know Wyatt but was hopeful he could be someone good for Joey. She deserved it. I got my trowel and dug a small hole in the center of the soil of the first pot and placed a small, light pink flower inside.

"We'll get this worked out," I said. I filled the second and third pots with flowers. I stood back and admired our work. "This looks better with every addition. I'm going to fill the watering can." I headed up to the office where there was the only outside faucet. Renovating one treehouse at a time was going really well. I returned to our work area to find Mom putting her big bag back into the car. I sprinkled water on each of the three plants. Seeing the beauty really did pick up my spirits. Soon enough I'd have to get going to figure out what happened to Violet. Judy was right. That was going to throw a big wrench into the pet parade.

"Get away from there," Mom said to Max. He had sneaked around the side of the steps to the garden stakes and had lifted his leg. I went over to see what Mom was concerned about. And right in the middle of the cute garden stakes was one of her garden gnomes. A little guy with a green hat, cherries on his head and holding a welcome sigh. Max was peeing all over it. "Chloe, look what he's doing. Can you keep him in check? He always seems to be bothering my gnomes. I don't know what's gotten into him."

I was doing everything I could not to bust a gut laughing. "We didn't agree to re-home your gnomes here." I used my watering can and gave it a shower to clean it off. Max looked at me, head down, eyes up, as if he was being scolded. I reached down to pet him.

"I know. But look how cute they are. They really jazz the place up. And he does fit right in with the cherry theme."

They do something, not sure jazzy is it.

"I can't wait to work on the other places. Making them look better will be really good for business. I should have done this long ago," Mom said.

I concurred. Having projects to spend my time on while I was in town really did give me some purpose.

CHAPTER FOUR

Max and I returned to the scene of the crime. If we didn't have answers soon, Pearl would be right. People in this town would ignite a firestorm of rumors and it would be all over for her business. Max trotted through the doorway as if there hadn't been a recent tragedy here. *Maybe he's remembering all of the good times he and Trixie had.* Pampering with Huckleberry scrubs. Manicures, massages. The works. I would prance too if I had received those treatments.

"Hi Buzz," I said. In high school Buzz and I dated for a while. We had become quite good friends after that. Max walked over and sniffed the spot where Violet had been. He looked up at me, curiosity in his eyes. I went over to Pearl and gave her a hug.

"Hey, there. And how are you doing, boy?" Buzz leaned over and gave Max a good scratching behind his ears. The entire back half of Max's body wiggled and he gave that big, goofy Muppet grin. "You come to check on Pearl?"

I went to the display case and retrieved two bottles of the huckleberry shampoo. "Yeah, plus I needed some supplies. This stuff smells amazing. I'm tempted to use it on myself."

"Right? I'm grateful that people spend more on their dogs than themselves. Keeps Pearl in business," Buzz said.

"But for how long?" Pearl chimed in. She went behind the checkout counter and got a bag for my purchase. "If Violet's badmouthing my place wasn't enough, as a final straw, she had to go and die right in my lobby." Pearl's eyes watered, and she choked out those last few words. She rang up my purchases and loaded them into the bag.

"Any word from Emerald Hills Police Department on the cause of death?" I asked Buzz.

He glanced at Pearl, not wanting to further upset her. He came closer to me and said in a whisper, "It looks like strangulation."

My hand went up to my throat. He shook his head yes. I looked over at Pearl and she busied herself arranging the products on the shelves. I went behind the counter and grasped Pearl's hand.

"We'll get to the bottom of this," I said. She looked up at me, tears overflowing her eyes.

"I didn't hate her and I'd never wish her dead," she blubbered.

I took her in my arms. "I know," I said and patted her back.

The bell on the door jingled and we all jumped. Max yipped. The tension was so thick we could cut it with a knife. Yes, we needed answers, and fast, so we could return to normal small-town life.

Everett Landon bustled through the door with a spring in his step. I looked at Buzz, who had a perplexed look on his face. Certainly Everett was aware that Violet had recently died in this lobby. "Hello, Pearl. What a great day!" Everett almost yelled. "I'm so excited to share some of my new products with you today." He lugged his large supply cases up to the counter.

"Everett, it's not a good day," Pearl mumbled.

He ignored her and began to unpack several bottles and line them up on the counter.

"Everett," Buzz said.

Everett stopped what he was doing and looked at Buzz, then Pearl. "What? Life goes on. You know Violet wasn't a favorite of mine. And I can't say I'm sorry to see her go. But nothing I can do about that now."

He picked up where he left off and emptied his bag onto the counter. A couple of the bottles rolled onto the floor. Max sniffed Everett's hand as he reached for the wayward shampoo bottle.

"Whose dog is this? Can you get him away from me?" Everett asked.

Max growled. Always the most accurate judge of character. Everett's crass attitude toward Violet and Max was not winning him any new business. Max got closer to Everett and his left rear leg began to raise.

"Max." I patted my thigh to call him over. Not that I wouldn't approve of him peeing on Everett, who deserved it. But probably not a good habit to condone. He tipped his head down and stopped mid-leg raise. "Max." He dropped his leg and came to stand right by me. He gave a low growl. *I agree, Max. A pet product supply salesman should totally be more of a dog person.*

"I'm sorry, Pearl," Everett conceded. "It must be hard for you that it happened here. But you have to admit, it's better for both of our businesses that Violet's gone. She'd been complaining for years how the huckleberry products tinted Sasha's coat purple. They do no such thing. I'm sure her negative reviews have cost me a lot of business, and you as well." Everett retrieved the bottles from the floor and arranged everything on the counter in preparation for his sales pitch. "Why don't I leave a few samples of our new product here? I'll come back again when you're ready."

Pearl didn't say a word, just sniffled assent.

"She'll call you," Buzz said. He went to the counter and helped Everett return the supplies to his storage case.

With everything packed, Everett practically skipped out the door. I felt another low rumble from Max as Everett passed by. If not for his excellent manners, Max would probably have taken a nip out of his calf.

Buzz went to the other side of the counter and put an arm around Pearl. "I'm sorry, hon. Everett's right, though. Maybe it would help to focus on the business to keep your mind off what happened to Violet."

Pearl nodded, picked up the samples Everett had left, and headed to the back room.

"That was rough," Buzz said when Pearl was out of earshot. "She's built this business up, and to have that happen is a serious blow. But we've got to go one step at a time. Hopefully, the pet parade tomorrow will cheer her up. It's the biggest driver of her business for the year."

"There's certainly no love lost between Everett and Violet. Do you think he had anything to do with her death?"

Buzz stared solemnly into my eyes. "Frankly, I don't know. I don't want to think so," he said.

Max started scratching himself again. I hoped it wasn't a nervous habit he was developing. Maybe another massage was in his near future. He'd been through some stress over the last year. I reached down to quell the scratching so he didn't hurt himself.

"I'm looking forward to the parade. It's always a fun time. Mom and I will be there with the pups." Maybe some year I'd see if one of Joey's grandkids wanted to enter in the parade with one or both of the dogs. Might be a hoot.

"I've got to head to the store to pick up the ice cream supplies Wyatt and I are handing out to the kids at the end of the parade." Buzz was at the door, ready to leave.

"I've heard a lot about Wyatt. I hope to meet him tomorrow. Let's go, Max." I attached his leash, grabbed my bag of supplies, and we followed Buzz out the door. I still had no more answers to the question of who killed Violet.

CHAPTER FIVE

The pet parade tradition had been going on almost eighty years in this small town. Every August, kids and their pets would dress up and head down Main Street. The only purpose was fun. When I lived here, we always watched the parade but never had pets. I was envious of the other kids who had dogs and now I had my very own. Max and I headed to Caroline's to pick up some coffee and treats, and then we were picking up Mom and Trixie. If I decided to stay in town, maybe Max could partner up with one of Joey's grandkids next year to enter the contest. I pulled into the parking lot and we headed inside. Max veered to the display table where Caroline had several boxes of her signature gingersnap cookies for sale. Today was almost as big of a business boon for her as it was for Pearl. I tightened the leash to keep Max by my side. His sweet tooth ruled him again.

He stopped in his tracks and looked at me over his shoulder, his eyes pleading. *Maybe later, buddy.*

Caroline was busy behind the counter serving two other customers. Max and I waited our turn. "Hi, Chloe. What can I get you two?" Caroline chuckled. She'd started keeping a small jar of dog friendly ginger treats behind the counter for our visits. She handed me one and I fed it to Max. He carefully chewed it with his good manners. He gulped and smiled big, waiting for another one.

"You're spoiling him. I'm going to get a couple of coffees and a box of your mixed pastries, to go." When Caroline's pastries were fresh, they were mouth-watering. "Mom and I are taking the pups to the pet parade later."

Drool dripped from the left side of Max's mouth. He sat next to me, every part of his body still, except his stubby tail. He was in a staring contest with Caroline, begging for another treat. "Max," I said. He didn't budge, one mission on his mind. I laughed. His persistence paid off. "OK, Caroline, one more treat, then we have to cut him off." Fat chance. He always got what he wanted. She came around the counter and put the treat on the floor for him, then gave him a scratch behind his ears.

"You'll have to look for my float in the parade. It took a lot of work, but it's so cute. It's a giant slice of cake. It's set up so that it covers a wagon. My great-niece is going to pull it. She'll also have her dog that will be dressed as a cupcake."

"That sounds adorable." Max whimpered. We ignored him and he raised his voice.

"That's it for today, little buddy. He smells good," Caroline said.

"I know. It's those huckleberry products I got from Pearl's. I think she used the scrub when he was there the other day. I picked up some shampoo too."

Caroline returned behind the counter and washed her hands. She loaded the six pastries into a box. "I couldn't believe when I heard Violet was killed. And in Pearl's lobby. That's horrible." Caroline put two of the ginger treats into a bag and tucked them into the box. Max watched her the entire time, not missing a beat. He'd have to share one of those with Trixie when we got to Mom's.

"It is. Violet made some enemies, but who hated her enough to want to kill her?" I asked. "Buzz let me know that the Emerald Hills PD is not having much luck in the investigation."

Caroline placed the pastry box into a carrying bag and set it in front of me. Max took a step closer and placed his snout at the very edge of the counter, continuing to eyeball her. "Sadly, there were several people that she wasn't afraid to go against, no matter the consequences. Her protests against that proposed housing development got her a lot of notoriety. The Emerald Hills TV news crew even came and interviewed her."

"I know that project has definitely divided this town. Many are in favor of increasing the tax base and modernizing. But probably more people are opposed and want to maintain this slower, country pace of life," I said.

"She also filed that lawsuit against Everett," Caroline said. She got two paper coffee cups and lids and began to fill them.

"What was that about?" I asked.

"Apparently she thought his products had given Sasha a rash or discolored her snow-white fur or something," Caroline said. She placed the lids on the cups and put them into a carrier next to the bag.

I pulled out my credit card and paid for my purchases. "That sounds like Violet. Every time she took that dog to Pearl's, she argued with Joey about paying for the services. And I don't think Pearl ever got over the fact that Violet treated that purebred dog like a mutt."

Caroline got a tray of bear claws and loaded them into the display case.

I gathered my purchases and juggled them with Max's leash. "It seems Violet brought conflict with her wherever she went."

"Thankfully, I was never a part of that. I'll see you later at the parade," Caroline said.

I waved, and we headed out the door to Mom's. That housing development was definitely a big deal in this town. Probably the biggest deal since the gold rush. It would bring a lot of jobs for a while and grow the town in ways that would forever change the landscape. Many people's livelihoods were on the line with it. It would only be good for the Treehouse Hotel. We could always use more business.

CHAPTER SIX

"**M**om, why don't you get the dogs and I'll carry the chairs?"

We'd parked at Pearl's so we could position ourselves center street for the best vantage point for the parade. I leashed up the dogs and grabbed our chairs out of the back of the car. I heard lots of happy voices that sounded like the kids and their pets were ready for the show.

This would be a nice break from the hotel for a bit. Mom and I had been putting in a ton of work, and the units had started to look pretty great. Time with Mom, now that I'd moved from her house into the Buttercup Bungalow, was also much more pleasant. Max and I had our own space—and a much needed respite. Now that Mom had adopted Trixie, Max had gotten a break from that little stinker. She and Mom had become fast friends. For that, I was grateful.

The parking lots filled fast for what was sure to be a whole town event. We wove our way through the maze of cars. In a back window, I spotted one of the signs Violet used for her protests when demonstrating against the development. I wondered whose car it was. As far as I knew, Violet was the only one who stood out there at the park with her signs. We arrived at the front of Pearl's and I set up our chairs on the sidewalk.

More parade watchers lined the streets. I loved that this little town did something as quirky as a parade for their kids and dogs. The larger neighboring towns even began to participate. It turned out to be a pretty big moneymaker for a lot of businesses. Mom and I took our seats and waited for the show to start. The pups dutifully laid down next to us.

"Mom, I'm having dinner with Joey tonight."

Her head snapped toward me. "Find out about that Wyatt guy. I hope things are progressing nicely for them."

I was pretty sure Mom would have made a great detective. She was incredibly curious about most everything.

I checked my watch. Crowds of people continued to fill in. It was getting close to starting time.

Buzz and Pearl arrived to claim the two empty chairs next to us. "Hey, you two," Buzz said. Max and Trixie scrambled to attention. Buzz chuckled. "OK, I meant Chloe and Mabel. But I guess I'll greet you both as well." He bent over and gave some hefty back scratches, to the pups' utter delight.

"I can't wait for you to see the float this year for my business," Pearl said. "I've been working too hard on it. I'm sorry I had to be so secretive the other day at my shop. I just wasn't ready to spill the beans."

This parade meant a lot of customers for Pearl, and she committed a lot of time to it every year. One year she had a fully decked-out *Wizard of Oz* replication.

Buzz's chuckles continued. "You should see our garage. It looks like a construction zone with glitter, crepe paper, and streamers every-where. Hey, there's Wyatt. I'll be right back. We're both handing out the ice cream to the kids at the end of the parade."

Just as soon as Buzz left, Judy arrived, strutting as if she was the queen of the world, the town her fiefdom. Her whole demeanor now that Violet was gone had become even more pompous, if that were possible. "Hello," Judy greeted with a formal parade wave. "This year is going to be the best yet." Max stood and looked at me, then looked at Judy. He looked back at me and approached Judy. She took a step back. "Get him off of me," she squealed. "Ugh, we have too many dogs in this parade. I'm so glad Violet's not in charge now. We need to have more cats. They're such better pets."

Max slightly lifted his right rear paw off the ground and looked at me with his peripheral vision.

I gave a shake of my head. That's all we needed. I patted my thigh.

He lowered his leg and sat, still on guard.

"Well, I have to go mingle. I am on the town council, after all. People expect me to be socializing," Judy said and darted away.

She continued down the sidewalk and met up with Buzz and Wyatt in front of the window next to Pearl's. Right behind her in big bold lettering was a sign that said Diamond Hills Development Company. How could I have not noticed that before? That must've been where Wyatt worked.

Mom leaned over and in a loud whisper said, "I really don't like her." Mom's directness was one quality I could use more of. She didn't waste time mincing words.

Max stood, barked, and wagged his tail, concurring. Judy really couldn't have been less sympathetic to Violet's death. I didn't expect her to be bawling, but at least show some compassion. Especially as a public figure, fake it, if nothing else. Did she have something to do with getting Violet out of the picture? It couldn't have been a better scenario for her.

"It looks like it's about to start," Mom said and started clapping.

I peered down the street and saw a 1959 fire-engine red convertible Corvette with Judy's husband Otis perched on top of the back seat. Flags whipped in the breeze from the side mirrors. Horns honked to signal the start of the show.

Buzz returned to his seat as we waited for the floats to arrive. Mom leaned over to him and in her loud whisper said, "Did Wyatt mention Joey?"

Buzz looked over Mom's head at me. I shrugged. "Um, no. Why would he?"

Mom sat back in her chair. "You know they're dating. They'll probably get married." She had already advanced the relationship several months or years down the road. I knew she only wanted the best for her kids. But this was pushing it. I would find out at dinner tonight just exactly how far this had gone. The last I'd heard, Wyatt had been dating Violet before she died. I just hoped he wasn't playing Joey for a fool.

Judy had roosted next to Otis in the lead car. She took it all in, obviously campaigning for mayor. Her stint on the city council had given her a platform to advance her political desires. She let no one or nothing stand in her way. Behind the lead car, the first float appeared with a little girl dressed in a Wonder Woman costume. She had a yellow Labrador retriever, grinning ear-to-ear, dressed in a Superman costume. And a black Labrador retriever dressed in a Darth Vader costume. The pets got just as big of a kick out of this as the kids, by the happy looks on their faces.

"My float's coming next," Pearl said. She clapped. "Look how good it turned out."

It was darned cute. Mom and I joined the clapping. Max stood up and lifted a paw toward Pearl's float. The front of the platform had a garbage can with a little girl, and a dog dressed in green, both peeking their heads out. The sign in front said *Sesame Street*. The back of the float had faux brick walls where Elmo and Cookie Monster were mounted. The commitment to these projects was serious. Next up, a wagon carried five pugs, each wrapped in a different-colored sweater with an M&M's label on their side. This parade was the highlight of my visit. Max turned and looked at me, wanting to join the fun. *I don't know, boy. I'm not sure we'll be here next year.* In the meantime, we were pretty busy fixing up the treehouses and solving the puzzle of Violet's death.

CHAPTER SEVEN

The din of the Smokehouse Restaurant made it hard to hear each other. Joey and I had gotten together a couple of times since I'd returned to town. I really enjoyed reconnecting with my sister. She always had a lot going on with her family. I was happy I could give her a breather once in a while. The place was hopping with the talk of the pet parade we had seen earlier that day. The joy of the kids and pets warmed the heart of even the most callous person.

"This is nice, getting some one-on-one time with my big sis," Joey said. For the longest time, I hated that reference. I was only the oldest by a few minutes of us triplets and somehow that put me in charge of the kids at home when Mom had to work. Now, I was happy to own it and help out in any way I could.

"It's crazy busy in here. We could have come another time so you could have worked and earned the tips."

Joey smiled warmly. "Nah, this is way better than any money. Wasn't that parade adorable? It gets better every year. It's one of the reasons I love this place."

I sipped my coffee. "Each float was cuter than the last. I might even enter Max and Trixie next year." I took another sip of my coffee.

"What? Does that mean you've decided to move back?" Joey almost squealed and bounced in her seat.

We placed the menus on the end of our table to signal to the waitress we were ready to order. "I'm seriously thinking about it. Now that I've moved from Mom's to the hotel, it's given me the separation to keep my sanity."

Joey gave a little finger wiggle to someone entering the restaurant. I looked out the corner of my eye to see Wyatt come through the door. He smiled big at her. I looked back at Joey, sure she blushed. She bowed her head and busied her hands with the napkin. "I would love it so much if you moved back. I don't get to see Zoe much, and I could really use a sister more prominently in my life." She kept her head down.

I had a giant grin on my face. It was clear that there was a spark between Joey and Wyatt. "I agree. And working on fixing up the hotel with Mom has been a blessing for me too. It's bringing back good memories of the projects Frank and I did together before he passed. I loved admiring the results when we had finished."

Joey lifted her head. She giggled, while continuing to fidget with the napkin. The waitress came and took our orders, giving Joey a reprieve from my quizzing. I took another sip of my coffee and slowly set the cup down. I folded my hands on the table.

"OK, so yes, I like Wyatt. There, I said it."

I held up my hand. "It's none of my business. But, how did you two meet?"

Joey snuck a peak at Wyatt across the room. Her pink cheeks returned. "His office is next to Pearl's. I was out on a walk one day and we almost literally ran into each other when I rounded the corner."

"You know," I started. "Mom already has you two married."

She sat back, a serious look on her face. "Chloe, I really have learned my lesson. If anything is going to happen, I'm taking it slow. If I marry again, it has to be for a final time. I have to be done with all the drama."

I saw movement again near Wyatt's table. Judy had entered the restaurant and joined him in the booth. "Well, that seems odd," I said.

Joey followed my gaze.

"Why would Judy be having dinner with Wyatt?" I continued.

Joey shrugged. "Probably something to do with that development he's working on. He's always so busy with it that he doesn't have time for much else."

The waitress arrived with our meals. We placed our napkins on our laps and dug in. The restaurant really honed their smoked meat process. Everything was mouthwatering. "He's probably not shedding a tear with Violet's departure. I bet she made a lot of trouble for him," I said.

Joey continued her solemn tone. "You don't know the half of it. Every time Violet marched at the property with her protest sign, another investor seemed to disappear. Wyatt was livid last week when the largest one pulled out."

I devoured my barbecued chicken dinner. I would have to get some take-out and keep a stash of this at home. Maybe even a morsel or two for Max. "She certainly wasn't shy about her views. When a couple of the newest treehouses were being built at the hotel, she chained herself to the trees, claiming they were crying and she had to save them," I said.

Joey slyly grabbed another peek at Wyatt. That girl was smitten. I was happy for her. If he treated her well, then they should be together.

"I couldn't stand her either," Joey said. "Every time she came into Pearl's I wanted to leave. About half the time, she had me in tears. I tried everything I could to avoid her."

Max and I had started our list of suspects for Violet's murder. Reluctantly, I had to put my sister there, as she was present when Violet died. Even as mad as Violet made her, I couldn't see her harming a hair on anyone's head.

"Does Wyatt have enough investors for the development to go forward?" I asked. The waitress arrived to refill my coffee and I waved her away. I would be up all night if I didn't quit now.

Joey sat her napkin on the table and pushed her plate back. "He had a couple of people that wanted to, but he wasn't sure their financing would come through. The last time Everett came to Pearl's to stock us up on products, he bragged how he was going to invest. He really wanted to be a bigwig and get out of hawking pet supplies. He was so mad when Violet kept badmouthing his huckleberry scrub. That had been his bestseller until she filed that stupid lawsuit for damages to her dog."

"Wow, it must have been bad," I said.

She shook her head. "Not really. When Violet brought Sasha in it looked like she had one scratch she'd given herself. There was no evidence it was because of Everett's products. But Violet insisted it was. Even if it wasn't, the damage to Everett's reputation, and his finances, was done. That only amped up her smug attitude. She felt like she always had to fight for the underdog, even if it meant making enemies."

The waitress placed our bill on the table. I agreed with Joey. Sister time was long overdue. Living so far away, I had missed a lot of family get togethers. Was this worth the move back to town? "This was wonderful. Thank you." I packed up my doggie bag with treats for my boy. I couldn't wait to bring him home a surprise and snuggle in for a puzzle, but my head throbbed trying to piece together the mystery of Violet's murder. I needed me some Max time so we could sort it all out.

CHAPTER EIGHT

The brightness of the yellow decor played well off the brown wood from the tree and treehouse. Buttercup Bungalow was one of my favorite units because of the prominence of the trees inside the building. One branch of the tree was situated to be used as a bench in the corner by a window. It made an amazing reading nook, the perfect place to peer out at the territorial views. Getting Mom up the stairs to this unit was also easier than most of the others. I was glad I decided to help with renovations so she didn't have to chance hurting herself scaling the entrances. I carried our decorating supplies up the steps and returned to the bottom to retrieve Mom. Max scurried behind me, supervising each part of the journey.

I took Mom's arm to support her climbing the steps. "I've got everything upstairs, Mom."

She pulled her arm away. "I can do it, Chloe." And she marched right up to the door without missing a beat. I stayed close behind, in case I needed to catch her. I hoped I was as spry and spunky as she was at her age. Somehow she managed to keep her wits about her and she was pretty good at getting around. I had definitely inherited her independence.

Max and I entered the door and scanned our project, assessing where to start. I had enough decorations for a room twice this size. "Mom, feel free to take a seat and point to where you'd like us to put the items."

She took me up on my offer and plopped down onto the tree trunk. "We really need a cushion for this thing," she said and patted it. "First, why don't you put the rug next to the bed. That way someone will have something warm on their feet when they get up."

I got the oval yellow and gray rug out of the bag and placed it parallel with the bed. Right on cue, Max settled onto it, christening it approved. He stood and started furiously scratching again. I wondered if that huckleberry shampoo was drying out his skin. I'd need to check with Pearl and see what else she had that might help.

"Did you bathe him? Why is he always scratching?" Mom asked. She got up and retrieved the yellow curtains from another shopping bag.

I looked at my boy. He shrugged. "I just did. Maybe it's the dry air," I suggested.

Max stood and went into the bathroom. What could he be doing? His bed and food were in the main living area. As I got to the bathroom he met me at the door with a piece of paper in his mouth. I should have known. I pulled it from him, expecting it to be a receipt from my decorating purchases. Instead, I found a label from the huckleberry shampoo. Why would he do that?

I peered over his shoulder and saw all of the labels from all of the dog supplies lying on the floor. What in the world? As I got closer, I saw all of the bottles still had labels, but different ones. I picked up one and looked at the back. The ingredients were definitely chemicals and not at all the natural, organic variety the other label advertised. These were the products I bought from Pearl the first time I took him to her pet spa. As far as I knew, Everett was the only supplier for these products in town, which meant one thing—Everett was scamming Pearl.

"Way to go, Max," I said.

Mom joined us in the bathroom doorway. "What did he do now?" she asked. "Oh, boy. Did he rip those labels off? I knew he ate paper. You really should keep a better eye on him."

Except Max had just discovered a piece to the puzzle of what may have been a motive for Violet's death. If she discovered Everett had been deceiving people with inferior products, her lawsuit against him was justified. I needed to get to Pearl's and find out what she knew about this. It might be news to her.

"Let's keep going here, Mom. We need to finish this so we can start on the Morning Glory Manor."

She returned to her perch.

Max looked at me and grinned. His tail wagged, showing his pleasure that he'd discovered another clue.

"So tell me what happened with Joey last night?" Mom prepared for a gossip recap.

I pulled the two lemon-colored lamps out of another bag. The base was almost shaped like the fruit and the shades had a diamond pattern of yellow and gray. The lights would also brighten up the natural darkness of the interior.

"We had a nice time. I realized how much I missed my sisters." Max got up and circled the rug. He eyed me, knowing what was coming next.

"That's why you should move back, Chloe. Just make your mind up finally and do it." Max approached me as I held a lamp in each hand. He nodded his head yes, in approval of Mom's plan. I think he'd finally gotten used to Trixie and would probably miss her if we left.

And the major league puzzle we had to solve kept us busy. It didn't hurt that he got to live in a tree. What dog wouldn't love that?

"I'm still thinking about it. There's a lot to consider."

Mom gazed out the window.

"Wyatt was at the restaurant too."

Mom jerked her head back to my direction. "Did you guys talk to him?"

I continued to retrieve our treasures from the bags and place them around the room. With each one, the place smiled a little brighter. "No. Actually, he was having dinner with Judy."

Mom stood and went to the night table to straighten a lamp. "What? Oh, maybe they were talking about his new development. That's all she can talk about. Like it's going to be her legacy or something."

I gathered up the empty bags and sat on the bed. "It's probably the biggest thing to happen in this town since the treehouses were built."

"It'll be interesting to see if it goes through, even after Violet's death. Her legacy was trying to preserve the natural beauty. We definitely have that with the treehouses. But a housing development? That's just too big-city for us," Mom said.

I looked at her, uncertain what her response to my idea would be. Ever since I had arrived to help her restore this place, I'd been thinking about what we could do to really secure the future business. "So, Mom. I want to pass something by you that I've been thinking about. Something that could really launch this place back into prosperity."

She tilted her head toward me. Max stood and mimicked her, ready for my brainstorm.

I gulped. "I'm thinking if we added a lodge and maybe a couple more units, we could really grow the business. The lodge could be a gathering place for a lot of events in town and we could advertise for out-of-town guests to have their meetings or events here."

Mom got up and circled the little room. She returned to the bench. "Hmm."

Seriously, that's all I got? "What do you think?"

Max barked three times. I took that as a yes from him.

Mom looked at Max. "I agree with him. It's a great idea, Chloe. I love it!"

I'd never gotten that resounding of an endorsement from Mom for any of my ideas. I got up and hugged her. Max joined in and leaned against our legs.

"OK. Let me call the permit office and see what we need to do." This would no doubt take some time. But it would keep me really busy here until I finished my work on the place.

CHAPTER NINE

Max and I wove our way through the variety of displays Caroline had in her store. The business seemed to be picking up, but she continued selling just about anything and everything that had nothing to do with coffee or pastries. Max beelined to the counter, ready for his treat. Caroline spoiled him at every visit with his favorite gingersnaps.

"Hey, two of my favorite customers," Caroline greeted. She wiped her hands on her apron and opened the dog treat jar.

Max politely placed a paw on the edge of the counter. Caroline retrieved his snack and placed it right next to him. He scooped it onto the floor and quickly nibbled it up. He expectantly returned his paw to the counter.

I laughed. "Never hurts to ask, right?" I rubbed Max's head. He looked at me over his shoulder, persistent in his quest. "Maybe later, boy. After our walk." He gently and obediently pulled his paw down. "Coffee, a bear claw and, of course, a couple of treats for my boy."

Caroline got one of the pastries from the display case and placed it in a bag. "Where are you going on your walk?" she asked.

Max slowly wandered to the other side of the hat rack. I suspected he was trying another angle to convince Caroline of just one more treat. If that was the case, I'd reward him for his ingenuity.

"Cedarbrook Trails. We haven't had much time to visit and I could use a change of scenery. Although, it's not much different than the treehouse landscape."

Caroline poured my coffee, put the lid on, and handed it to me. "It really is beautiful there. I'm so torn between keeping that pristine natural place or the housing development. One reason I live here is the peaceful nature. But that development would be great for my business and the town coffers."

Max was now nowhere in sight. I expected him to emerge on the other side of the counter right next to Caroline. That boy was clever.

"I agree. It's given me some ideas about how to improve the business at the hotel. I really want to set Mom up well by the time I'm finished renovating. If my plans pan out, we'll really have a great family asset on our hands." I stood on my tiptoes to see if Max had made it around the counter. "Do you see my boy over there?"

Caroline looked to her left and shook her head no. OK, he'd wandered off to who knew where? Probably trying to get someone else to share their treats. I went to the end of the counter near the hat rack. A familiar voice wafted through the display. I didn't see Judy when we came in. She was seated alone at a small table tucked into a corner. She must have been on the phone.

"Don't worry. With Violet out of the way, you and I are totally in the clear." Her head tilted toward the window with her right hand held to her ear.

Max approached Judy's table with stealth moves. With her head in her papers she didn't see him. I spotted his prey. A plate full of gingersnaps right in front of Judy. I clicked my tongue to get his attention. He took two more steps in Judy's direction. She continued in her oblivion to her surroundings.

"Wyatt, trust me. With the two of us together, there's no stopping us," Judy said.

I couldn't believe my ears. Judy and Wyatt were having an affair. They didn't even try to hide it at the restaurant last night. Joey would be crushed. But if he was a scoundrel, better to find out now. I didn't want to be the one to tell her. She had such a sparkle in her eye last night that I hadn't seen in a long time.

Max's head almost touched the plate with Judy's cookies on it. She turned, and seeing him for the first time, jumped back. "Get away, you mutt," she yelled. She slammed her phone down and shooed him with her hands. "Go away! How rude!"

Max growled. He shook his head from side to side. "Sorry about that. He's usually so polite to everyone he meets. Come here, Max," I said. He stood his ground and raised a paw. He tapped Judy's leg.

She squealed and scooted her chair further into the corner. "He's attacking me. Get that vicious animal away from here."

I took hold of Max's collar. "I'm pretty sure he's just after your cookies," I said. I tried to pull him toward me. He refused. He pawed at her leg again. I smiled.

Judy moved her plate out of Max's reach. "It's not funny. He could really hurt someone," she said.

Max, confident his message was received, obediently sat by my side. "That must be cat hair on your pants. I think he's just smelling the fur."

Judy looked down and swiped her pant leg. "I don't see anything. And that's why I have cats. They would never be so aggressive toward me and steal food off my plate." Judy had at least five cats, probably more by now. They were more unruly than Max could ever be. Judy had promised her cats would be entered into next year's pet parade now that Violet's "no cats" rule was null and void. It would be a three-ring circus.

"We're headed out anyway," I said. Max relented and let me lead him away from the table. His stealth hearing was another tool in our puzzle-solving box. "We're going to explore the Cedarbrook Trails. I haven't been there since I came back. I'm sure it's changed a lot."

Judy scoffed and waved us away. "Enjoy it while you can."

Max whimpered. *Yes, buddy. We have to compare notes. I can't tell who's coming and going in this mystery of Violet's death.* Exploring the trails would help us clear the fog in our brains to figure out what was really going on. I grabbed my purchase from the counter and waved goodbye to Caroline. Max whimpered again. "I'm as surprised as you are, Max. I never would have pegged Judy to be having an affair with Wyatt. Otis is going to be devastated. And once they've been found out, her stint on the city council will surely come to an end, her reign over this little town finished. Let's go."

CHAPTER TEN

Max perched on the passenger seat of my car, navigating us to one of the trailheads at Cedarbrook Trails. We couldn't wait to explore the ten miles. Although today, maybe we'd just do a short stint to warm us up for a longer one at a later date. I parked, and we got out of the car. I took a deep breath to inhale the fresh, clean air. "Ah, some much needed clearing, Max." He wagged in agreement.

The signs offered multiple paths for every desire. We didn't have much time today, so we chose the shorter Cherry Hills loop. I leashed him up and we headed down the path. This place was a haven for outdoor lovers and had something for just about everybody, whether you were on a horse, a bike, or just your own feet. Thankfully, it was still cool enough and there was plenty of shade to rest when needed. The fir and pine forests spanned as far as your eye could see.

We began our ascent to the first hill. It was a gradual incline, but I started to breathe a little heavier. Max trotted along as if this were a total breeze for him. I needed to get into better shape so this wouldn't be our last trip. We reached the peak and I bent over to catch my breath. After about thirty seconds I took a seat on a bench to take in the view. The Emerald Hills valley in the distance teemed with wildflowers of every color. This time of year was primetime to enjoy so much in bloom. However, the fall colors rivaled this show when the leaves began to turn. Even the snow in winter provided a wonderland of beauty. I was pretty sure Max would adjust plenty well to a move here. But could I?

My life had been my own for several decades. Before my husband Frank passed, it was just the two of us. We played hard and adventured every moment we had. A return to this town meant a whole new era in my life, one I needed to prepare for.

"Alright, boy, let's keep going." I stood and Max sped ahead. We ventured down the other side of the first hill. The view changed to be the forest floor. Less light permeated the treetops. The foliage and underbrush thickened on both sides of us. I was thankful the trails were well-worn so we wouldn't get lost.

A *clop-clop* noise came from the opposite direction. I briefly stopped to confirm the sound wasn't just my fast-beating heart. I wasn't sure how Max would react to seeing a horse. He began to prance as he spotted the large animal, raising his knees in rhythm with the horse's clopping. I strained the leash to slow him down. We moved to a wide spot on the side of the trail where we could wait for them to pass. Max obediently sat to watch the parade. The horse and rider slowed a bit as they went by, waving.

I returned the wave and Max lifted his front leg, offering a greeting. Could he get any cuter? The more we were together, the more I noticed his genius and engaging personality. Cats schmats. Judy didn't know what she was missing by not having a dog. I waited until the distraction had sufficiently disappeared. Max and I returned to the trail. I began walking and he wouldn't budge. I gave a little tug and he leaned back, more solidly attached to the ground.

"What is it, Max?" I bent over and examined his legs. Was he injured? Or had he come into contact with poison oak? I had a small first-aid kit in my backpack. I hoped it wasn't something worse. I gently cradled each leg and felt for an injury. Nothing appeared wrong.

He stood up, turned ninety degrees to the right, and sat back down. What? Was I getting the silent treatment for some reason? I moved and stood in front of him. I crouched down and gave him the once-over again. Had I missed something the first time? "I don't get it, Max." I stood up and peered down at him with my hands on my hips. He craned his neck around my left leg. I turned around and saw them. Large red spray-painted Xs marked several of the trees about ten yards off the path. I knew what that meant. Someone had already been here to identify which trees were coming down to make room for the development. I had no idea it was this far along. I was actually skeptical that it would go forward. This town wasn't one to adapt to a lot of changes, especially one as big as the housing project. There were a lot of hoops to jump through, albeit less now that Violet was gone.

"Looks like we may have found another piece to the puzzle. Let's keep going to see where this leads us," I said.

Max pranced again, much more buoyed than I felt. We continued for about a hundred yards to another wide spot in the trail. I carefully led Max through the brush to avoid any danger.

The farther we went from the main trail, the more red Xs we discovered. I stopped and shook my head. But I couldn't deny what was right in front of us. We returned to the trail. A sign told us we were halfway through the Cherry Hills loop. We continued on for the second half of our trip. We wound through a mix of open and dense areas as we approached the edge of the Cedarbrook Trails property.

If my internal navigation was accurate, we should be near the hotel property. We searched for an opening to again venture off the main trail. My heart sank. I saw Buttercup Bungalow in the distance. I was sure this was the hotel property. I counted over twenty trees marked to be taken down. Max approached the nearest one and lifted his leg, expressing both of our displeasures for what we had discovered. How could Mom or I not have known this was happening? This development was enormous. It would more than triple the size of this small town. No wonder Wyatt was trying to get more investors. Making this happen was going to cost a pretty penny. And that was just for the building expenses. The inevitable lawsuits would rival that bill. With that kind of money on the line, people could do unspeakable things. If Violet saw what was happening, she would be turning in her grave.

"Max, we have to find out what's going on. My dream for expanding the treehouses might just have been dashed. I hope it's not too late." Max jumped on me and slurped my cheek, ready to take on our foe.

"With her town council position, Judy's the only one who could have pushed this through so quickly without us knowing about it." Max growled. His eyebrows angled down and his jowls dipped. One mention of Judy changed his whole demeanor. "Let's go, boy." We jogged the remainder of the way to our car, re-energized for our mission.

CHAPTER ELEVEN

I was steamed that I hadn't put the clues together earlier about Judy's plans. She was a person who always had to have top-of-the-line things in her life. Nothing wrong with wanting the best, but to scheme your way to it was another story. According to Joey, she found Judy standing over Violet's body when she discovered them in the lobby at Pearl's. Judy's personality made you bristle, but was she devilish enough to want Violet dead? Would Violet's threats to tie up the development for years in court for environmental issues cause Judy to snap? I placed my hand on Max's back as he sat in the copilot seat of the car. The warmth of his body and his steady pulse calmed me. He looked at me, his eyes concerned for my well-being. "Thanks, boy." His stubby tail thumped.

We pulled into Pearl's parking lot. I reached in back, grabbed my purse and the bag with the jar labels that Max had found. Max and I were becoming frequent visitors at Pearl's. My boy deserved every pampering treatment they had. So far he'd had a massage and a bath with the huckleberry scrub. When we solved Violet's murder he would be treated to the rejuvenation package, including the Moroccan oil rub down and Dead Sea salts scrub.

We entered the lobby where the familiar bell jingled. Joey was the cashier today, another nice surprise. She and Pearl had their heads together. Joey gave a wave and a huge smile when she saw us. Max ran toward her as she crouched for a big hug. "Hey buddy, we don't have you down for an appointment. To what do we owe this surprise visit?" she asked.

From behind the counter, Sasha, Violet's poodle emerged. "Oh, Sasha's here," I said.

Pearl approached her and stroked her thick fur. It looked exceptionally nice, probably an extra special cut from Pearl. She had never liked how Violet treated Sasha. With her pedigree, that dog could have regularly placed very well at national dog shows. "I'm taking care of her for now. She can finally be treated in the manner she should have been all along." Pearl hugged Sasha and closed her eyes.

Sasha greeted me. Her fur was as soft as newborn baby hair. The poodle curls looked as if they'd been individually styled. She had a large pink bow clipped to the back of her neck. "She looks great," I said.

"Did you guys need some more supplies already?" Pearl asked.

I looked at Max. He came to my side. "No, I have something I wanted to share with you. I hope it's not a surprise. But I'm afraid it will be." I took the bag of labels and dumped the contents onto the counter.

Pearl looked at me. She frowned and shook her head. "What is this?" she asked.

I straightened out of a few of the labels. "For the last couple of days, Max has been scratching more than normal. I thought maybe his skin was dry, so I applied some of the moisturizer. But it seemed to get worse."

Pearl picked up each label, examined them, and lined them up on the counter. She shook her head again. "What's this? Everett has been scamming me. Not just me, but all my customers." Pearl's shoulders droop with frustrated defeat. "Chloe, I can't believe this is happening to me. After everything else I've been through."

I continued. "I went into the bathroom and saw all of the labels for every product I bought from Everett had fallen off the bottles and were on the floor. Underneath each one was another label. I looked closer and saw the ingredients on the labels still on the bottles were mostly chemicals. I think Everett relabeled these so he could charge more."

Pearl ambled over and plopped into one of the waiting chairs. Max approached and rested his chin on her knee. His brown eyes radiated love. She rubbed his head. "I'm so sorry, Max. How could I have missed this?" Pearl's voice cracked. She treated every customer as a part of her family and the dogs like they were her own kids.

I shoved all the labels back into the bag. "I'm sorry, Pearl," I said.

Pearl stood, her fists balled, her back straightened. "I knew he always wanted more than this pet supply business. But to do that to defenseless animals for his own gain? That's so wrong." She grabbed the bag from me, crumpled it up, and barged through the door to the back room.

I took a seat in one of the guest chairs. Max joined me in the adjoining seat to my right. "After everything she's been through, I hated to have to tell her that." I put my arm around Max and he leaned into me. "Until we can solve the mystery of Violet's death, her business will keep suffering."

Joey joined us in the waiting area, sitting in the chair to Max's right. Her eyes were red and puffy. "Are you OK?" I was so intently focused on those labels I missed how upset she was.

She turned away. "Yes."

"Joey, what's going on?" I reached past Max and placed my hand on her shoulder. Max put his paw on top of my hand.

Joey chuckled. "You'd think working in a dog spa that I'd have a dog by now. But my kids and grandkids keep me busy enough." She tipped her chin down. "I don't want to be a burden."

I waited.

"Brady was arrested for stealing," was all she could get out before losing it. She bent over. "He tried so hard. I thought it was getting better. With his priors, this won't be good." Joey's oldest son had been a troublemaker from day one. Not major stuff, usually nothing to harm people. But vandalism, petty theft. He'd been taken on as an apprentice at the local mechanic shop.

"I'm so sorry, hon. What happened?" I got up, faced her, crouched down, and held her hands. Max stood and hugged her with both of his front legs.

"I don't know exactly. When Violet was last in here, she accused him of stealing something from her. She had hired him to do some yard work. He claimed he didn't take whatever she said he did."

I retrieved a handful of tissues from the counter and pressed them into Joey's hand.

She dabbed her eyes and nose. "The thing is, Chloe, I believe him this time. I don't know why. I just have a feeling."

I lifted Joey's chin to look into her eyes. "Trust your instinct. I mean, definitely find out the truth. But why would he mess up a good thing he had at Marv's Mechanical?"

Max made the quietest bark I'd ever heard from him. We both laughed. "And that's from someone who has great instincts. He knows," I said and stood up.

"You're both right. When I got the call, I was scared it was worse." Joey took all of the tissues and muffled her cries. Her family certainly put her through the ringer. "I mean, theft is bad. But what if Brady got mad at Violet for accusing him? What if he had something to do with her death?"

"Joey, trust that he didn't. From what Max and I have uncovered, he had nothing to do with it. Just take one step at a time."

She stood and wrapped her arms around me. The stakes for Max and me to solve this murder raised every day.

CHAPTER TWELVE

Max and I had a messy enough puzzle on our hands with Violet's death. I now also had to find out what was really going on with this housing development. At every turn, new information was revealed that indicated there was a lot of behind-the-scenes maneuvering. I couldn't let Mom find out that there were complications. She was so excited about the possible expansion of the hotel, already planning names for the two new treehouses. Could Wyatt prevent our future expansion? Or worse, cause us to tear down some of our existing units? I took a deep breath and entered the city hall building. I had to keep my focus neutral until I knew there was something to really be upset about.

The clerk behind the counter asked, "How can I help you?"

I stepped up to face her. "Is this where I find out about getting a building permit?"

"It sure is," the clerk continued. It said Theresa on her name tag. "What type of building are we talking about? And where?"

I set my thick file folder on the counter. In case I'd need to reference some prior hotel documents, I'd brought all that I could find. There was still a lot of bookkeeping to go through to get it all organized. I hoped everything I needed was in there.

"We're looking at expanding the Cedarbrook Treehouse Hotel by a couple of new units and adding a lodge," I said.

Theresa tilted her head and looked at me over the top of her glasses. "Are you Chloe?"

I stared at her, compelling my memory to kick into gear. "Yes, I am. My mom, Mabel, owns it. I'm in town to help her for now. I'm sorry. I haven't been here much lately. Do I know you?" With the size of this town, it wouldn't take me long to get reacquainted with every single resident.

She shook her head. "Nah, we haven't met. I'm friends with your niece, Brittany. She said you were back helping."

I smiled. It never hurt to make more friends in this town, especially ones that could help sort out the mess with the hotel. "When I called earlier, the person I talked to mentioned that there was a hold on any new permits for the hotel right now. Can you tell me why? I'm not aware of any issues."

"Sure, just a sec." Theresa left the front counter and went to a room that was filled floor to ceiling with filing cabinets. She pulled open a couple of drawers and inserted placeholders where she removed some large files. She lugged them out to the front counter and plopped the dust buckets down in front of me. "Sorry about that. Paper seems to be a magnet for dust. We try to keep the room aired out. It helps some." She thumbed through the piles of paper, taking several items out and placing them to the side. Satisfied she had found what she was looking for, she turned around a stack of papers to face me. "There's a couple of things. Right here, it looks like someone named Violet had filed an appeal against the approval of the original construction. It looks like that was resolved. But in the event expansion ever came up, she submitted another appeal to preempt anything from even being approved to start." Theresa pointed to a location on the paper with Violet's signature.

I took a step back and held my nose to prevent a sneeze. "Well, how do I get that removed so we can submit our proposal?" I lost the battle and sneezed three times. My eyes watered. I pulled a tissue from my purse to stifle the flow.

Theresa returned the first stack of papers to the folder and closed it. "That's the type of thing that has to go to the town council for review. They actually have a meeting later today. Agenda items have to be submitted a week in advance to be discussed. But you could speak during the public comment period if you want."

I held my nose to stifle any more sneezes or I'd never get through this conversation. "Is that all I have to do? Just show up? I don't have to get permission from anyone?"

"Nope, that's it," she said.

I smiled. That step seemed pretty simple. I'd make some notes beforehand so that I could succinctly make my pitch to proceed with our proposal. I was buoyed by that news. "You said there were a couple of things. What's the second one?" If it was as straightforward as the first, I'd soon have some good news for Mom.

Theresa held a second stack of papers close to her chest. "This one looks like a much bigger deal." She fanned out the paperwork in front of me.

I looked up at her for an explanation. "Can you help me understand this? I'm not sure what I'm looking at." I furrowed my brow and concentrated on the first piece of paper she pointed at.

"This one here is an application for that new housing development. This is the really big project that's going to change this town forever." She looked up at me slowly to see my response.

I still wasn't tracking her line of thought. "OK."

She pointed to a second piece of paper that showed approval to proceed with clearing land. Public land. The portion of the trees that Max had spotted at Cedarbrook Trails. And to clear the portion that overlapped onto the hotel property. Her finger slid over to the signature line where I read Judy Livingston. "The paperwork to begin the official development has been submitted and approved. This is on the council agenda today for them to give the final consent to start clearing the land."

I took a step back, stunned. With as little fanfare as humanly possible, this would do exactly as Theresa said. Change this town in ways that nobody could imagine or approve. And I bet it had happened right under everyone's nose. Judy wasn't having an affair with Wyatt. She was directly involved in shoving this development forward. She must be one of his investors. I couldn't let this happen. Even if I didn't get approval to expand the hotel, I had to stop this destruction. Violet's shenanigans and protests had been a constant burr in the saddle of the town council. But could her opposition to the development be the reason someone killed her?

CHAPTER THIRTEEN

A smattering of people filled the rows of chairs facing the dais. The town council meeting was scheduled to start in about fifteen minutes. I took a seat in the back row. I needed to observe the process before I stepped to the microphone and made the pitch of my life. Judy looked like she was holding court chatting with her fellow council members, throwing her head back laughing like she was in the catbird seat. I looked down at the notepad on my lap. I made notes of what I wanted to say when my time came to speak. I ticked through each point in my head. I had no idea what would happen after that. I hoped the decision wouldn't take long. That would put a huge damper on the hotel future and my planned stay in town. The audience chairs continued to fill as the clock ticked toward the top of the hour. The council members meandered to their seats as the mayor gaveled the meeting to order. He began with introductory comments to review the agenda topics for the day. Most of the council busied themselves with papers in front of them, heads down. The mayor announced the first agenda item.

"Today, we're going to name as Milly Kennedy day. We want to recognize Milly for her work with homeless kids." The mayor read a proclamation honoring Milly and her tireless efforts for the food and clothing drives. When he finished reading, he got up and descended to the podium in front of the dais. An elderly woman, who I assumed to be Milly, stood and met him in the front of the room. We all clapped as the mayor handed Milly a certificate, shook her hand, and they turned for a picture. Milly and her family filed out of the room. The mayor then returned to his seat. He shuffled papers and moved on to the next topic, the upcoming election for mayor.

"Since I'm stepping down as mayor at the end of my term, we'll soon have a new person filling this seat." He turned and looked at Judy. She sat tall, soaking it all in. "The original candidates on the ballot included Judy Livingston, Violet Connelly, and Anthony Warren. With Violet's untimely death, we're down to two people vying for the position. Judy shook her head yes. The smug look on her face assumed victory. *Well, we'll just see.*

The mayor continued, "Since we're so close to the election, we don't have time to alter the ballots to remove Violet's name. We will proceed as is."

"That's OK. Everyone knows she's gone," Judy butted in. All heads swiveled toward her. She slumped in her chair, appearing a bit embarrassed by her interruption.

With an audible sigh, the mayor continued to the next agenda item. "Next up we have our public comment period. We've also got a sizable topic at the end of our time today. We'll take a fifteen-minute break after our public comment time before we finish our meeting."

I gazed around to see if anyone else was going to speak. Immediately, a young man sprang up and approached the podium. He introduced himself and launched into a diatribe about the importance of the town's history. He insisted the council recognize and vote to change the name of the town after one of his distant relatives. He wanted it called Herbold's Burgh after Edward Herbold. Judy chuckled, which drew a dirty look from the mayor. She stifled her laugh and covered her mouth with her hand, still shaking her head no. If she was going to be mayor, she'd have to work on her poker face.

The mayor thanked the young man, who proudly returned to his seat. The mayor inquired if there were any other speakers for today's meeting. I rose from my seat and made a beeline to the front of the room. I placed my notes on the podium and stilled my shaking hands by holding its sides. I slowly panned my eyes to each of the council members, arriving lastly at Judy. Her smile turned upside down. Her jovial demeanor had disappeared.

"Thank you for the opportunity to comment. My name is Chloe Carson. My family owns the Cedarbrook Treehouse hotel." I placed my finger where I had left off in my notes. "I recently learned of an appeal that was previously submitted by Violet Connelly preventing any future development at the location." I paused and swallowed, preparing for a strong closing statement. "I respectfully request that appeal be denied." I cleared my throat, relaxed my shoulders, and dropped my arms to my side. I quickly glanced up from my notes. Most of the council rummaged through their paperwork, shifting papers left and right. I looked down and continued. "We plan to submit a proposal to expand the hotel by adding two additional units and a lodge. The units would be consistent with what we have now. The lodge would be designed to provide a venue for many of the larger events that currently have to be held in our neighboring city, Emerald Hills. Our town would have a place where we could gather, and by drawing business, help support the town budget. Thank you for your consideration." Talk money and everyone listened.

"Thank you for the comments, Chloe. I acknowledge Violet disrupted and damaged this town and our business future for a long time." Judy had jumped in ahead of the mayor's comments. She spoke as if she was giving a stump speech. "I appreciate you bringing this to our attention."

Was that it? Was I dismissed? "You're welcome." I waited.

The council began to talk amongst themselves while Judy and Councilman Ford guffawed.

"So what are the next steps?" I asked.

"Well," Judy began, further speaking over the mayor. "We take the matter under advisement. After we thoroughly analyze, we'll decide how to proceed." She turned back to Councilman Ford. They continued their laughter.

"Thank you, Chloe." The mayor quickly resumed his role. "As Judy said, we'll let you know if the appeal is removed. If it is, you're free to proceed with your proposal. Once the permit department receives that, we'll have another public comment period."

I straightened my notes and smiled. "Thank you, and if I may, I would also like to comment on the proposed development."

All talk stopped. Judy glared at me.

"Of course," said the mayor. "This is your time."

Judy continued her efforts at intimidation. She placed both hands on the surface in front of her and leaned forward. "What about it?"

I gulped and grabbed the podium again, prepared for an even more hostile response to my comments. "I have discovered the planned development includes the taking of property from the hotel. I want to let you know that I'm planning to submit an appeal to prevent that."

Judy grinned. "You can't do that. The development is claiming eminent domain. It's in the long-term interest of the town, more than your little treehouses are."

I straightened my papers and looked down. Did I have any chance to stop this? We would barely be able to keep enough units in operation, let alone expand, if this development went through. "I understand that. However, I don't believe the proper steps were followed, and I will still be submitting my paperwork," I said. I was hopeful but not optimistic. With Judy ruling the roost, anything could happen.

"We'll now take a fifteen-minute break before our last topic this meeting. All adjourned until then." The mayor slammed the gavel down. Judy and Councilman Ford had their heads together, an intense conversation happening. I had no idea if my comments would make a difference, but I had to try.

I turned and headed down the aisle toward the exit for a breather until the council resumed after the break. What would I tell Mom?

If that appeal wasn't lifted, that would be a huge blow to the future of the hotel. Or worse. If that development took over hotel property, that might ultimately be the end of the legacy. Just as I pushed open the council room door, a hand pulled it from the other side. Standing right in front of me was Wyatt.

CHAPTER FOURTEEN

"Hi, Chloe." Wyatt held the door for me to leave. I didn't move. After an awkward pause, he stepped around me and continued into the meeting room. I turned around to see him sit in the front row. Judy gave him a friendly wave. He nodded his head. Wyatt set a paper roll and his large briefcase on the chair next to him and clicked the latches open. I returned to my seat in the back row for this portion of the program. It was about to get interesting. Although this was a public meeting, most people never had any idea of the significant business done by government that affected their lives, all done in plain sight. Wyatt retrieved a large file folder and snapped his briefcase shut. The mayor looked at the clock and signaled the rest of the council to return to their seats. Time felt like it stood still as the mayor opened the second part of the meeting.

"Our last agenda topic for this meeting is final approval of the proposed Diamond Hills housing development. I'm going to read into the record the specifics of the project. Then we will do a review of the plans and wrap up with a review of the financial details." The mayor described the specifics of what had been requested. The four hundred and twenty acres to be developed, the combination of mixed use and housing, the number of units, and the tentative timeline. If this went forward, those houses could be occupied as early as the following summer. "Before I continue, Councilwoman Livingston, as I understand you are an investor in this development, you will need to be recused."

Judy rose from her seat and proceeded to the front of the audience, taking the opposite end of the row from Wyatt.

Wyatt slouched in his seat, his arm draped the chair back next to him. Judy assumed a similarly confident posture. The two of them had schemed together for the biggest deal in this town since the gold rush over a century ago. People would do anything for money.

The mayor finished recapping the proposal. He looked up at Wyatt. "Mr Smith, I'm going to turn the meeting over to you. Would you now please conduct a review of your plans as submitted? We're especially interested in those areas where your proposal is dependent upon other parcels in the area."

Wyatt nodded and proceeded to the podium. He plopped the file down on the table next to him. He unrolled the property map and placed it on an easel to the side of the room. With a laser pointer he described the perimeter of the four hundred and twenty acres. I saw from my vantage point a portion of hotel property was clearly part of their plans. Max's identification of those trees was spot on. It was apparent that the Cedarbrook Trails property would be partially taken over by the development as well.

Judy stood and leaned toward the chart. She looked at Wyatt and returned to her seat. "Do I understand you correctly that the project you've proposed will cover part of the Cedarbrook Trails as well as the Cedarbrook Treehouse hotel?" she asked. Her smile was long gone, replaced by a frown. She was furiously writing notes.

Before the Wyatt could respond, the mayor gaveled three times. "Councilwoman Livingston, you are recused. Therefore, you are not allowed comment during this period."

Wyatt continued, "That's correct. It's all there in the approval papers," he replied, gesturing toward the council.

Judy ripped a single sheet of paper from her pile she had taken with her. She turned it around and held it with both hands for Wyatt and the council to see. "You mean this one?" she asked.

The gavel slam startled her. She looked at the mayor and he glared back. Receiving the message, Judy sat back in her seat.

"Please continue, Mr. Smith," the mayor said.

"If that's the project approval letter, then yes," Wyatt replied. He shifted his weight between his feet. "So with that approval, I'd like to proceed with the final piece of financial review. If you'll go to section three, I'll start with the investor data." He grabbed a notebook, placed it on the podium, and flipped through the pages.

Judy held up her hand. "Whoa! Before you do that, we need to look at this approval. The original application didn't say anything about taking the other properties mentioned. Is there another approval letter in this package with those details?"

The mayor crossed his arms and shook his head, losing the battle to keep Judy in check.

Wyatt pointed to the piece of paper in Judy's hand. "It's all in the original right there." He turned and pleaded with the mayor to shut Judy's comments down. But I didn't think there was any way that bulldozer would stop now.

"We may have to take this topic back to a work session. It looks like there's some discrepancy. Judy, your signature is on the approval. What am I missing?" the mayor said.

Judy turned the piece of paper around, looked down, and gasped. "That's my signature. But I would never approve taking the additional property for this project. I value the history and natural beauty here too much to do that."

Wyatt pulled out another piece of paper and waved it. "Since we obviously have the approvals, I'd like to proceed with the financial review." He looked at the mayor and received his assent to continue.

Judy slumped in her seat and shook her head. She was clearly blindsided by his proposal. I couldn't understand why she wasn't more upbeat. Wouldn't a bigger development benefit her even more from a financial standpoint?

Wyatt continued, "I admit, we've certainly had our challenges with investors. With Everett Landon pulling out at the last minute, we had to scramble. But we finally have a solid set on board. Enough to proceed."

Judy returned to her full-seated position. The dollar signs in her eyes now gleamed. The almighty buck overruled any objection she had to the proposal taking property from other owners.

The mayor continued, "Why don't you walk us through phase one?"

"Of course," Wyatt said. "The initial location of phase one is solely on the property initially purchased. This way, we can provide for those who need time to adjust to the expansion by the time we are in phase two."

Judy wiggled in her seat.

"Can you run the numbers for us on the total and then by phase?" Councilman Ford asked.

Judy preened as Wyatt detailed how she would be profiting. I didn't begrudge her a return on her investment. But when it came at the expense of others, that was too much.

Wyatt flipped through the notebook again. "I'm now looking at section four. The final financials approved by the bank."

The council headed over to that portion of their documents and the mayor nodded to proceed.

"What is this?" Judy stood and shook the paper at Wyatt.

"Order," the mayor said and gaveled.

"You thief!" Judy yelled again, pointing at Wyatt.

The mayor gaveled several times. "Councilwoman Livingston. Please contain yourself or you'll be excused."

"But Mayor! Wyatt Smith has not only forged my signature on the approval, but he's scammed me out of my share of the project. The financials show him and his investors as the sole owners. My contribution and ownership are nowhere to be found. How could you!?" Judy's voice now escalated.

Wyatt returned all of his papers to his folder. "Your honor, Councilwoman Livingston is obviously upset. And I feel she's too close to this project to cast a final vote. I respectfully request she be removed from the remainder of the meeting."

"With Violet out of the way, we were home free. How dare you take advantage of my good nature for your own benefit. Without me, you'd be nowhere. I know you wanted Violet gone because she threatened to out your illegal dealings. I can't prove it, but I'm sure you killed her." Judy plopped in her chair, dropped the papers, and buried her head in her hands.

"Councilwoman Livingston! For the last time, conduct yourself in a professional manner or you will be removed." The mayor's face reddened. No wonder he wanted out. This amount of drama in a small town? He probably ran for the position thinking he might only be involved in the occasional ribbon-cutting ceremony. The mayor dropped the gavel and threw his hands in the air as surrender.

It had now dawned on Judy that she had been Wyatt's pawn in his diabolical scheme. But he was in much deeper than just scamming people out of their money. I had to act quickly to alert Buzz.

I returned to the room and approached the mayhem. "I've already called the police. Wyatt, I know you were the last person to see Violet alive. You were overheard having an argument with her at the same time she was scheduled to pick up her dog from grooming. And the next thing we know, she's dead in the lobby of Pearl's."

He shook his head. "You don't know what you're talking about. That troublemaker was bad for this town and its future. This development is the best thing to happen in the last century."

"Can you explain why you had one of Violet's protest signs in the back seat of your car?" I continued, grilling him like I was a professional interrogator. I shakily moved further toward the front of the room. Was I taking my life in my hands in the presence of an alleged murderer?

He shook his head and hurried down the aisle to the exit, leaving his briefcase behind. "You don't know what you're talking about. I did you all a favor."

The mayor jumped up and sprinted after Wyatt. There might just be a take down in the lobby of city hall. As one of his remaining official acts, the mayor tackled Wyatt. I heard sirens in the distance.

Judy had her head down, sobbing. I felt confident the development as we knew it would never see the light of day. Just like Wyatt after he was convicted.

CHAPTER FIFTEEN

It had been a few weeks since the council meeting. They had done right by Violet. A portion of the Cedarbrook Trails had been dedicated as a dog park. It was quite the sight to see all of those pups running their hearts out in this space. Mom and I strolled the walking path along the perimeter as Max and Trixie romped with some new friends. This was such a great way for them to expend a bunch of pent-up energy. With all of my time attending numerous town council meetings to chauffeur the hotel expansion proposal through the process, Max had been antsy to get out. He would certainly be ready for one of Pearl's classic dog massages when he was done. He deserved that, and more, for helping solve Violet's murder.

Mom kicked a pebble. "I'm so mad I didn't see through Wyatt's slimy exterior before he hurt Joey. I'm usually a pretty good judge of character."

The dirt path was beginning to get a little muddy due to a recent rainstorm. We continued our walk, dodging mud puddles. "Nobody saw through it. That's how it is with those shysters. They're so slick, they even convince themselves that what they're doing is right, or for the greater good."

Trixie bounded over to Mom, who reached down to pet her. I was grateful Mom had her as a companion since I'd moved out of her house and into the hotel. "It's just too bad Violet had to pay with her life before we discovered it."

I called Max over so we could leash them up and head out. "I'm just glad Max was able to find some clues that led me to the answers. If he hadn't seen those trees marked for destruction, Wyatt may have gotten away with it."

Mom clasped Trixie's leash to her harness and we headed to the exit. Our pups' tongues lolled far out of their mouths. The rest of the dogs converged on us to say goodbye. I reached down to pet a couple. This place would definitely be on our frequent visit list.

I got the water and bowls out of the car to give the dogs a quick drink. They slurped them dry.

"Chloe, what's the big surprise you mentioned?" Mom asked.

I loaded the dogs into the back seat. "Actually, I have two."

Mom and I got in and buckled up for the ride home. "Well, don't keep me in suspense. What are they?"

I looked at her before I started the car. "We've been approved for the hotel expansion. We can add those two new units. So start thinking of names. And the lodge has also been approved as part of it."

She squealed. Max and Trixie jumped up and started barking. Everyone approved of the plans. "OK, you guys, settle down." They stopped barking but continued bouncing around the seat. I had no idea how they still had any energy to move at all. I started the car and headed out of the parking lot.

"With all of that space we can host larger events, which means more money for the hotel. This is really going to bring in new business to help us and the town too. I've already got plans to market to Emerald Hills and beyond. It's a pretty big project, but I'm ready."

"Did you just hint at the second surprise?" Mom's voice caught in her throat as she placed a hand on my arm.

I shook my head yes and looked at her. Tears formed in her eyes. The dogs stood and started barking again. I was fully convinced they understood humans. "Yes, Mom. I'm moving back."

"Oh, Chloe." She was speechless, not an easy feat to accomplish with my mom.

I turned into Mom's neighborhood. "It's the right time. Starting a big project at the hotel, it makes sense for me to be there."

"My family is finally becoming whole again. Now, all I need is Harrison. Maybe you can convince him." She removed her hand from my arm and placed it in her lap. "Would you talk to him?"

I hesitated. Never say never, but I couldn't see any path forward to Harrison's return to town. He and his family were firmly established elsewhere. A visit, maybe. But completely moving back? Although, maybe closer in another town could be a compromise. I'd see what I could do.

I pulled into Mom's driveway to deposit her and Trixie before Max and I returned to the hotel. I couldn't wait to collapse with my boy and settle in for a huckleberry vodka and a new puzzle, one that didn't involve someone dying.

"Yes. I will. And I'll have to take a road trip so I can get all of my things and put my house up for sale."

"Chloe, I don't remember when I've been this happy. Thank you."

I gave her a big hug. Max reached into the front seat and put both paws around her for a hug too. I got out and escorted them to the front door. I had no idea what I was getting myself into with a permanent return to this town and overseeing a major construction project. But what is life, if not an adventure? And this would be a whole new world for Max and me.

Hear From Max

Max tells his side of the story. Scan the QR code below with your device's camera to find out the scoop straight from the pooch's mouth.

NEXT RELEASE - BUTTERCUPS AND BETRAYAL

Chloe's newest project with the expansion of the hotel leaves her little time for a new love, let alone solving the mysterious death of the newly-hired, snooty museum curator, Bartholomew Higgons. Even so, she ends up smack dab in the middle of the murder and mayhem.

Partnered with her loveable cocker spaniel Max, they find themselves mired in a sticky situation. As Chloe and Max investigate, the clues lead to deeper secrets and complex relationships amongst the suspects. The plot gets thicker when a coveted museum treasure is stolen and the bingo scholarship money disappears.

Can the dynamic duo untangle the truth between disgruntled business partners, spurned romantic partners, and blackmailing bingo players before one of their beloved family members are arrested for murder in ***Buttercups and Betrayal***?

Scan the QR code below with your device's camera to order now.

THANK YOU

Thank you for reading **_Violets and Vengeance._** Reviews are crucial for helping other readers discover new books.. If you want to share your love for this book, please leave a review for other readers. I'd really appreciate it!

Scan the QR code below with your device's camera to leave a review.

About the Author

Sue Hollowell is a wife and empty nester with a lot of mom left over. Not far from her everyday thoughts are dreams of visiting tropical locations. She likes cake and the more frosting the better! Scan the QR code below with your device's camera to follow her author page on Facebook.